Toothless!

by Jenny Dobbie
illustrated by Craig Smith

D0320103

Characters

Lucy and her dog, Barney

Grandad

2

Contents

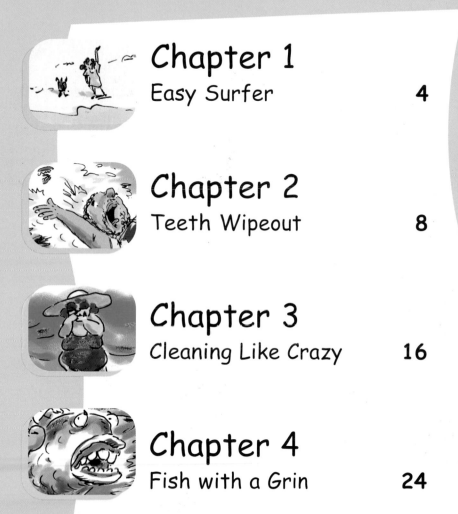

3

Chapter 1

Easy Surfer

Lucy's grandad loved to surf. He could ride the tube all day long! Grandad was a surfing legend. He had a room filled with trophies. He had won them in surfing competitions all over the world.

"Surf's up! It's eight foot and pumping!" he'd say. Then he'd jog to the water with his surfboard under his arm.

Paddling out to catch the waves sometimes made Grandad tired. So Lucy locked herself in her inventor's workshop. Next day she had invented something just for him.

"An automatic paddling surfboard! Cool!" gasped Grandad. He gave a big, white, toothy grin. "Lucy, you're the best inventor! No more paddling for me!"

Lucy had invented lots of things. She had
invented a gadget called *Doggie's Little
Helper* for her dog, Barney. It found Barney's
buried bones for him. And she had invented a
machine called *Crazy Cleaner*, for her
brother, Sam. It followed him around
cleaning up his mess.

All of Lucy's inventions had names. "This one," she told Grandad, "is called *The Easy Surfer*."

"Wicked name, Lucy," Grandad said. He was so excited he wanted to take *The Easy Surfer* for a test run straight away.

Chapter 2

Teeth Wipeout

When Grandad and Lucy arrived at the beach, Grandad raced down to the water. He hopped onto *The Easy Surfer* and set the control to 'paddle'. Then he headed out to where the waves were breaking.

"Watch me!" Grandad shouted to Lucy, as he rode a wave on *The Easy Surfer*.

Next, he set the control to 'fast paddle' and headed out to the big swell. He went way, way out from the shore.

"Be careful, Grandad!" shouted Lucy, as he surfed into shore.

Grandad grinned his big, white, toothy grin and zipped back out to catch another wave. "This is awesome! Check this out," he yelled.

Grandad set the dial on *The Easy Surfer* to 'paddle'. Then he put his hands on each side of the board. Slowly he lifted his legs straight up into the air.

Lucy stared, amazed. Grandad was doing a handstand!

"Grandad," yelled Lucy, "look out!" A gigantic wave was breaking just behind him.

"No worries," called Grandad, still standing on his hands. He pushed the dial with his nose. "I'll just set the dial to 'paddle fast'. I'll be out of here in a jiffy!"

Uh oh! Grandad had pushed the dial to 'reverse'. He was heading backwards into the wave!

"Whoa!" yelled Grandad, as he shot up the crest of the wave and flew high into the air. His arms and legs flapped madly.

"Look out below!" he shouted, as he fell into the churning surf. The waves tossed him about until finally he was dumped onto the beach.

"Wipeout!" spluttered Grandad, as he dragged *The Easy Surfer* up the beach.

"Grandad, are you OK?" asked Lucy.

"I'm fine," said Grandad, as he wiped the water from his face. He felt his mouth. "Oh no! I've lost my false teeth!"

Everyone on the beach searched for Grandad's false teeth. A boy found a gigantic pair of orange undies. The lifeguard found an old, rusty shopping trolley. But no-one could find Grandad's teeth.

"It's hopeless. They're lost forever. I'll have to get a new set," grumbled Grandad. "I hate getting new teeth. They're always so uncomfortable."

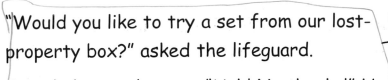

"Would you like to try a set from our lost-property box?" asked the lifeguard.

Grandad turned green. "Ugh! No thanks!" He sighed, "I'd better go ring the dentist."

"I know," said Lucy. "We'll get Sam's *Crazy Cleaner* to search for your teeth. It will find them."

Grandad beamed. "Great idea, Lucy," he said.

Chapter 3

Cleaning Like Crazy

Grandad and Lucy wheeled *Crazy Cleaner* down to the beach. Lucy set its dials to 'underwater' and 'pick up'. She pushed it into the water and turned it on. *Crazy Cleaner* chugged through the surf.

"Now we'll find your teeth," said Lucy.

"Is it supposed to spurt out steam like that?" asked Grandad. Steam was pouring from *Crazy Cleaner's* engine.

"Oh no! Something's wrong," said Lucy. "Look! It's heading up the beach!" *Crazy Cleaner* was chugging over the sand towards them.

"Watch out!" shouted Grandad. They ducked, as *Crazy Cleaner* threw a hat at them and then an umbrella.

Crazy Cleaner rumbled along the beach. It grabbed towels, surfboards and whatever else it could find and then hurled them away again.

"Take cover, everyone!" yelled Grandad, as a beach chair came flying through the air. "It's going to explode!"

Crazy Cleaner didn't explode. Suddenly, it stopped still and sat hissing quietly. Lucy tiptoed closer to take a look.

"Be careful, Lucy," said Grandad, following her.

"It's broken," she said, fiddling with the dials.

"Never mind, Lucy. Thanks for trying," said Grandad. He gave her a gummy smile. "I think I'd better get a new set of teeth."

Lucy patted Grandad on the back. "Don't worry, Grandad. I've got another idea. I just need to make a few changes to *Doggie's Little Helper.*"

Next day, Grandad and Lucy arrived at the beach, with an armful of fishing gear.

"Why do you want to go fishing, Lucy?" asked Grandad, as he dragged the fishing boat into shallow water.

"To find your teeth, of course," said Lucy.

"How are you going to do that?" asked Grandad, climbing into the boat after Lucy.

"You'll see," smiled Lucy. "It's a surprise."

The boat bobbed up and down over the waves, as Lucy and Grandad headed out to sea.

"Are we there yet? Is this the spot?" asked Grandad, staring into the water.

Lucy pulled a map out of her pocket and studied it. "Yes, this is it."

Grandad grabbed his fishing rod. He put a prawn on his hook. Lucy grabbed her fishing rod. Then, she pulled a metal box from her pocket. She tied it to the end of her fishing line.

"Isn't that *Doggie's Little Helper?*" asked Grandad. "How's that going to find my teeth?"

"It used to be *Doggie's Little Helper*, but I've fixed it. Now it finds false teeth instead of dog bones," said Lucy.

Grandad's mouth fell open. "Awesome, Lucy."

"I've worked out that your false teeth have drifted to somewhere near here," said Lucy.

"And that thing's going to find them! Wicked!" cried Grandad.

Chapter 4

Fish with a Grin

Grandad and Lucy dropped their lines over the side. They fished for an hour. Grandad caught seven fish. Lucy caught seven plastic bags!

"I don't get it," said Lucy, as she checked her invention. "This thing looks OK. I don't know why it's catching plastic bags. I'll try again."

They fished for another hour. Grandad
caught eight fish. Lucy caught eight
car tyres!

"I don't understand," sighed Lucy, scratching
her head. "Something must be wrong with it."
Lucy fiddled with her invention. She
unscrewed bolts and twisted wires. She
adjusted a tiny dial. "There! That should do
it. Now, I'll find your teeth, Grandad."

Lucy dropped her fishing line, with her invention on the end of it, over the side of the boat.

Grandad's shoulders drooped. "I don't know, Lucy. I think it's hopeless. We'll never find them," he muttered. "I've lost my lovely, white, sparkling smile forever."

Just then, Lucy felt something tugging on her line. "I've got something!" she yelled.

Grandad looked. A huge fish was splashing and thrashing on the end of Lucy's line. "It's a fish, Lucy! A beauty!"

"I should be catching teeth, not fish!" said Lucy frowning, as she hauled it in. The fish landed with a thud in the bottom of the boat.

"What a whopper!" yelled Grandad as he put his foot on it.

"I hope you didn't break my invention," Lucy said to the fish. The fish grinned back at Lucy.

"Grandad! Look!" cried Lucy.

Grandad's eyes nearly popped out of his head. "The fish is wearing my teeth!" he shouted.

Grandad hugged Lucy. "You're the best inventor ever!" He grabbed his false teeth from the fish and put them in his mouth. "That's much better." Grandad gave a dazzling smile. "Lucy, I've got the coolest name for your invention."

"What is it?" asked Lucy.

Grandad chuckled. "Well, Barney's bone-finding invention was called *Doggie's Little Helper*. This invention finds teeth so we should call it *Grandad's Little Helper*!"

Glossary

adjusted
changed slightly

automatic
able to move by itself

crest
the top part of a wave

drifted
carried along by water

inventor
a person who thinks of and makes something new

jiffy
a very short time

legend
a person who is famous
for doing something well

swell
a long, unbroken wave

test run
the first try

tube
the hollow part of a
breaking wave

Jenny Dobbie

I wish that I owned some of Lucy's inventions like *Crazy Cleaner* and *The Easy Surfer*. If I did I would set *Crazy Cleaner* to 'clean house', grab *The Easy Surfer* and race down to the beach.

It would be great fun zipping in and out of the surf and riding the tube. I might even try a handstand! Everyone would want a turn on *The Easy Surfer* — including Grandad!

But perhaps he'd better leave his teeth at home!

Craig Smith